LOOK AND FIND®

SNOWMAN

Illustrated by Jerry Tiritilli
Cover illustration by Alyssa Mooney

Louis Weber, C.E.O.
Publications International, Ltd.
7373 North Cicero Avenue
Lincolnwood, Illinois 60712

Ground Floor, 59 Gloucester Place
London W1U 8JJ

Customer Service: 1-800-595-8484
or customer_service@pilbooks.com

www.pilbooks.com

Manufactured in China.

8 7 6 5 4 3 2 1

ISBN-13: 978-1-4127-4643-4
ISBN-10: 1-4127-4643-4

Once upon a Christmas, I made a whole bunch of new friends as I helped them get ready for the holiday. Can you find me in the square as the villagers get their preparations underway? Can you find my friends, too?

Jenny

Lee

Mark

Michael

Kevin

Claire

Scotty

Chris

Deck the halls with boughs of holly! There's no time like Christmastime for putting up lots of decorations. These folks are really getting into the spirit of the season. Can you find these decorations? Do you see me?

Boughs of holly

The treetop angel

A snowman ornament

A drum ornament

A jingle-bell wreath

A candy cane

A snowman snow dome

An angel centerpiece

The reindeer that live in the North Pole have a very important job each Christmas. But when the reindeer aren't busy pulling Santa's sleigh, they like to have some fun! Can you find these familiar faces among the reindeer games? Do you see me, too?

Dasher

Dancer

Prancer

Vixen

Comet

Cupid

Donder

Blitzen

My friend the Tooth Fairy must be flat broke! The kids in this classroom are losing their teeth left and right! See if you can spot these kids who are missing their front teeth. Can you find me, too?

Scott

Silvester

Sally

Sandy

Simon

Suzannah

Sean

Sidney

Christmas Wish List

Michael - football
Chris- two front teeth
Jennifer - doll
Mark- two front teeth
train
sketball

Holly & Ivy - four
front teeth
Kim - puppy
Eric - bicycle
Lizzy - tap shoes
Marge- $E = mc^2$

The big city is full of the sounds of Christmas. People are laughing, taxis are honking their horns, and above that noise is the sound of bells ringing. Can you hear them? After you have found me, look for these treasures that shoppers are taking home.

A red bicycle

A television

A dolly

A puppy

A robot

A globe

A panda bear

This wrapped gift

A piano

LE GRAND PRIC

Up on the rooftop, the reindeer pause... while Old St. Nick delivers some special toys to little Nell and little Bill. He's checking to see if they have taken good care of their toys. Do you see him? How about me? And what about these toys?

A hammer

A train

A ball

A dolly that laughs and cries

A guitar

A rubber duckie

A bicycle

A jump rope

Here's a little town that means business when it is time to decorate Christmas trees! How lovely are these branches? Can you find my favorite ornaments? Then see if you can spot me!

Dog bone

Pink ornament

High-heeled shoe

Slice of pie

Wrench

Button

Lollipop

Music note

Panda bear

Santa Claus is comin' to town, and he always checks his list twice to make sure he hasn't made a mistake. He also keeps track of who was naughty and who was nice all year. Can you find four kids from each list? Can you find me, too?

Naughty

Naughty

Nice

Nice

Naughty

Nice

Naughty

Nice

Jingle bells! Oh, what fun it is to ride in a one-horse open sleigh! Everyone seems to be enjoying a sleigh ride today. The air is filled with the sound of harness bells. There are lots of other bells around, too. Can you spot these? Do you see me?

A green strap of jingle bells

A southern belle

A bellhop

A cowbell

A bell choir

A church bell

A belly flop

Bundle up and head back to the village square to see if you can find these funny things.

❑ A dog dressed like its master
❑ Two snow officers
❑ A singing jailbird
❑ A huntsman who's found a "fox"
❑ An invisible pet
❑ A crazy eight ball
❑ "Saw"-berry shortcake
❑ A leaky customer

Lots of things went wrong while decking the halls! Can you find these accidents?

❑ A wobbling ladder
❑ Two people slipping
❑ A toddler toppling a poinsettia
❑ A runaway sled
❑ Faulty wiring
❑ A guest who forgot her dress
❑ A tinsel fight
❑ A pie in the face

It's almost time for Santa to deliver his toys! Can you find these games the reindeer are playing before they head out?

❑ Marbles
❑ Checkers
❑ Pin-the-tail-on-the-reindeer
❑ Jump rope
❑ Baseball
❑ Hopscotch
❑ Cards
❑ Video game

Report back to the classroom and look for these eight disasters.

❑ Finger painting
❑ A bad science experiment
❑ A frog down a collar
❑ A bowl of soup on a head
❑ A worm in an apple
❑ A kid stuck to his chair
❑ A bookworm
❑ Ants in some pants

Head back downtown and look for these city things.

❑ Three taxicabs
❑ Three traffic lights
❑ Eight street lights
❑ 27 silver bells
❑ Six "Santa" stocking caps
❑ 11 wreaths